S0-BUY-244

written by
DARCY WHITECROW AND
HEATHER M. O'CONNOR

illustrated by
LENNY LISHCHENKO

Second Story Press

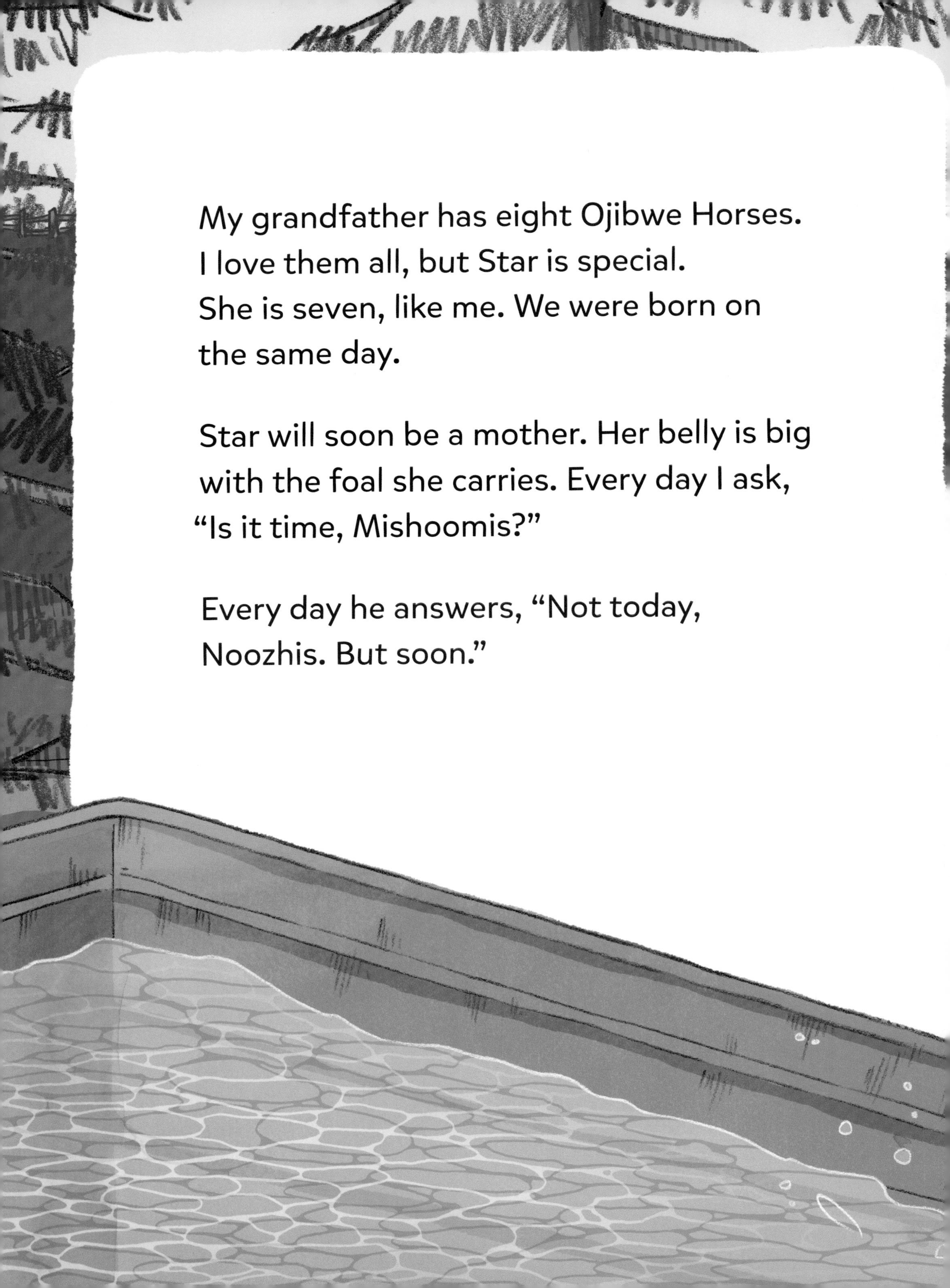

My grandfather has eight Ojibwe Horses. I love them all, but Star is special. She is seven, like me. We were born on the same day.

Star will soon be a mother. Her belly is big with the foal she carries. Every day I ask, “Is it time, Mishoomis?”

Every day he answers, “Not today, Noozhis. But soon.”

“Where did the horses come from, Mishoomis?”

Grandfather has been telling me stories about the horses for as long as I can remember so that one day, I can tell them, too.

Grandfather’s eyes crinkle up. “I have shared this story with you so many times. Tell me how it starts.”

I laugh. “It starts with *your* grandfather.”

Grandfather smiles and ruffles my hair.

"When my grandfather was a boy, herds of
Ojibwe Horses ran in the woods, like the deer.
In winter, when the wolves were hungry and
the ice was thick, they helped our people
travel, haul wood, and go trapping.
Elders say they were always here.
The horses were small, but strong."

"Like me?"

"Like you."

The next day, I ask again,
"Is it time, Mishoomis?"

"Not today, but soon."

The horses amble over. I give each one a scratch and a carrot. I don't want them to know I have a favorite.

Star noses me for the special treat I have just for her.

"What happened to the herds, Mishoomis?"

"By the time my father was a boy, the world had changed. Our people didn't need horses to haul wood or run traplines anymore. They used snow machines."

"Why?"

"You feed a snow machine only when you use it. A horse needs food and water every day."

"Like me?"

"Like you."

The next day, I help Grandfather groom the horses.

“Is it time, Mishoomis?” I ask.

“Not today, but soon.”

Star’s belly is wide and round. As I brush, her baby pushes against my hand.

“Mishoomis, look!”

Grandfather nods. “Seems you are not the only impatient one.”

“Soon, Little One,” I whisper.

To help us wait, Grandfather tells the rest of his story.

"Each year, the herds grew smaller until the thunder of hooves in the forest faded away. No one knows why. By the time I was a boy, there were only four Ojibwe Horses left at Lac La Croix. They slipped in and out of the woods like ghosts. My favorite was a bay mare with one white stocking."

“One winter, some men came and took the horses away. I never saw them again. I was seven.”

“Like me?”

“Like you.”

“I learned years later that the horses were taken across Lac La Croix to a place where they could run free. The mares were bred with a mustang stallion. Over time, the little herd grew big, and host farms here and to the south took in small groups.”

"Growing up, your mother never knew the horses. I didn't want you to grow up without them, too. That's why I decided to breed Ojibwe Horses myself. Star was our first foal. She arrived the same day as you, my first grandchild."

"When I grow up, Mishoomis, I'm going to raise Ojibwe Horses, too."

Grandfather pats my hand. "I would like that."

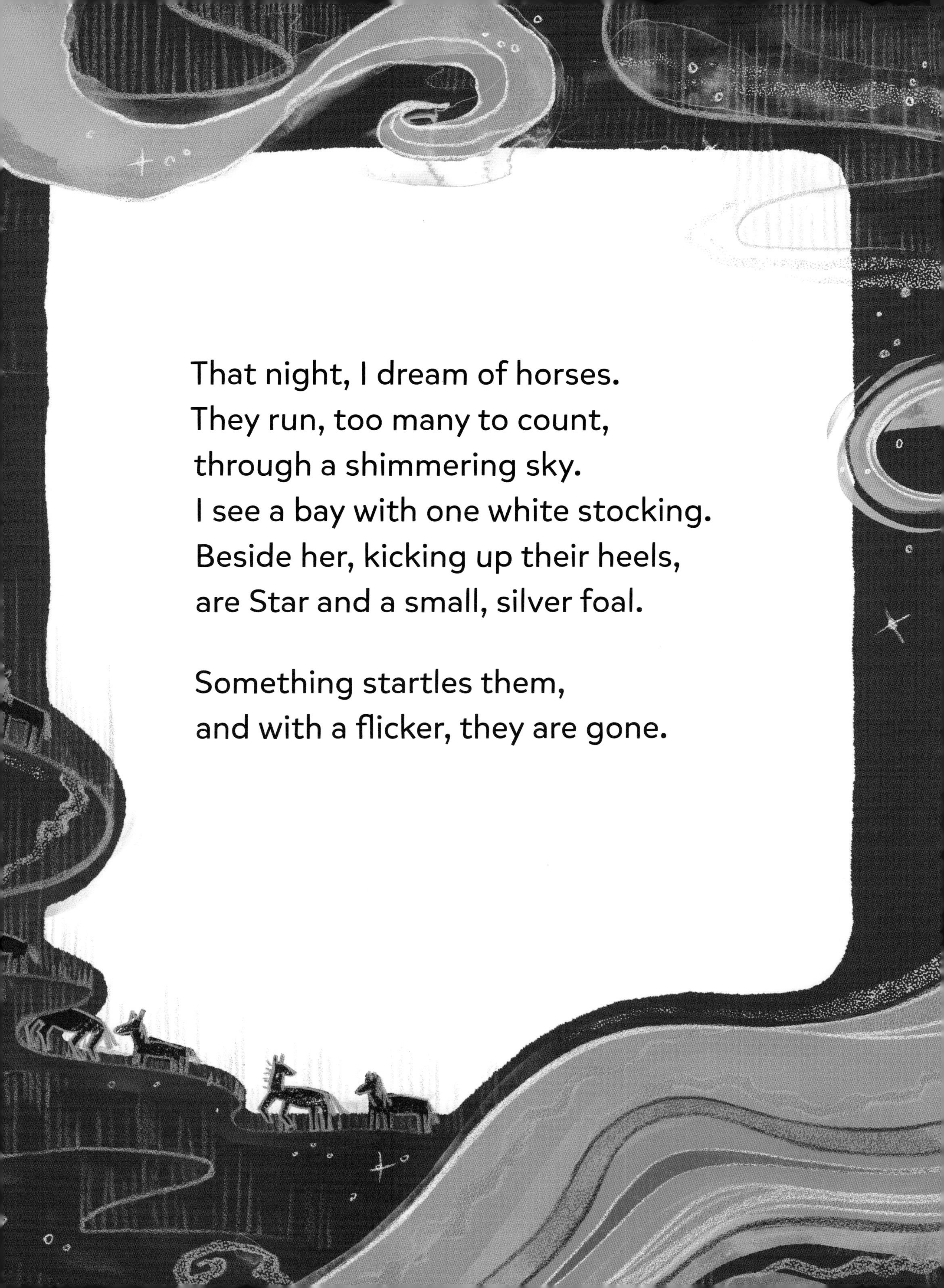

That night, I dream of horses.
They run, too many to count,
through a shimmering sky.
I see a bay with one white stocking.
Beside her, kicking up their heels,
are Star and a small, silver foal.

Something startles them,
and with a flicker, they are gone.

I open my eyes. Grandfather has come to wake me.
“It’s time,” he says.
Grandmother Moon rides high in the sky, lighting our path to the barn.

Star lies in the hay. And beside her...
a beautiful foal, as silvery as the dawn.
She lifts her head and looks at me.

I tell Grandfather about the foal in my dream.

"Perhaps she was whispering her name to you," he says. "Shall we call her Wiijibibamatoon-anangoonan?"

Runs with the Stars. I like the sound of that.

Star noses her baby.
Wiijibibamatoon-anangoonan pushes up
on two wobbly legs, then falls.
Star nudges her once more.
This time the foal's legs hold her up.

"Hello again, Little One," I whisper.
"Soon you will be big and strong, like me,
and we will run with the stars together."

AFTERWORD

The Ojibwe Horse, also known as the Lac La Croix Indigenous Pony, was bred by Ojibwe people living around the western part of Lake Superior. It is one of two Canadian horse breeds. (The other is the Canadian Horse.)

Once, thousands of Ojibwe Horses roamed the boreal forests of what is now Northwestern Ontario and Minnesota. By 1977, only four remained in the wild. Bizhiki, Lillian, Dark Face, and Diamond lived in the woods around Lac La Croix First Nation, next to Quetico Provincial Park. The government called them a health hazard and planned to destroy them.

Fred Isham, who once lived at Lac La Croix, came to their rescue. He and three friends roped the four mares, loaded them into a horse trailer, and drove them across the frozen lake to Bois Forte, Minnesota, where they were bred with a registered Spanish mustang called Smokey.

As the herd grew, dedicated people in Canada and the United States took on breeding groups of six to eight horses. The population now stands at about 175.

Today, these smart, friendly horses are often used in tourism, equine therapy, and cultural heritage programs. They're also popular saddle horses. In February 2018, Lac La Croix First Nation welcomed home its own breeding group—five mares and a stallion. It was a happy day.

To learn more about the Ojibwe Horse, visit the Canadian Encyclopedia or the Ojibwe Horse Society websites.

ACKNOWLEDGMENTS

Darcy and I would never have met without a research grant from Access Copyright, the Artist in Residence Program at Quetico Provincial Park, the Quetico Foundation, and the Ontario Arts Council. Heartfelt thanks to Anne MacLachlan, Jill Legault, Jason Blier, and Trevor Gibb (Ontario Parks), Chief Mike Ottertail (Lac La Croix First Nation), translator Kelvin Morrison, and experts Kimberlee Campbell, Lesley English, Joyce Young, and the Ojibwe Horse Society. Thank you to my dear friends Ruth and Cameron Walker, the Halls Island Artist Residency, and the amazing team at Second Story. And finally, thanks to my family. You are the best story I have ever written.

ABOUT THE AUTHORS

DARCY WHITECROW is Ojibwe and Dakota; he is a member of the Seine River First Nation band in Northwestern Ontario, where he lives. Darcy practices traditional lifestyles like trapping, fishing, and ricing, as well as traditional spirituality in both the Midewiwin and Sundance traditions. With his partner, Kim, they have started a non-profit, Grey Raven Ranch, where they have been raising and caring for Ojibwe Horses for the past decade to help preserve the breed and the tradition of symbiotic interaction with the Ojibwe people.

HEATHER M. O'CONNOR is an award-winning children's author and freelance writer based in Peterborough, Ontario. Her first picture book, *Fast Friends*, won the Ruth and Sylvia Schwartz Award and was a finalist for the Blue Spruce Award, the IODE Jean Throop Award, and the Shining Willow Award. She first learned about Ojibwe Horses while writing for the Ontario Parks blog and quickly became obsessed.

ABOUT THE ILLUSTRATOR

LENNY LISHCHENKO is not a boy. She is an illustrator, graphic designer, and comics maker who will never give up the chance to draw a good birch tree. Ukrainian-born and Canadian-raised, she's interested in telling stories that people remember years later in the early mornings, when everything is quiet and still. She is based out of Burlington, Ontario.

To Darcy, Kimberlee Campbell, and Mike Ottertail, who told me the story.
And to Anne, who sent me to them.
—HEATHER M. O'CONNOR

Library and Archives Canada Cataloguing in Publication

Title: Runs with the stars / written by Darcy Whitecrow and Heather M. O'Connor ; illustrated by Lenny Lishchenko.
Names: Whitecrow, Darcy, author. | O'Connor, Heather, 1960- author. | Lishchenko, Lenny, illustrator.
Identifiers: Canadiana (print) 20210298596 | Canadiana (ebook) 20210298677 | ISBN 9781772602388 (hardcover) | ISBN 9781772602401 (EPUB)
Subjects: LCGFT: Picture books.
Classification: LCC PS8645.H548 R86 2022 | DDC jC813/.6—dc23

Editor: Kathryn Cole

Photo credits
Page 30 (top): Ontario Parks (middle and bottom): Kimberlee Anne Campbell
Page 31: Ontario Parks

Printed and bound in Canada

Second Story Press gratefully acknowledges the support of the Ontario Arts Council and the Canada Council for the Arts for our publishing program. We acknowledge the financial support of the Government of Canada through the Canada Book Fund.

Published by
Second Story Press
20 Maud Street, Suite 401
Toronto, Ontario, Canada
M5V 2M5
www.secondstorypress.ca